THE SNOOPY SHOW

TIME FOR THE VET, SNOOPY!

by Charles M. Schulz

Based on *The Snoopy Show* episode "All's Fair, Snoopy"

written by Scott Montgomery

Adapted by Patty Michaels

Ready-to-Read

Simon Spotlight

New York   London   Toronto   Sydney   New Delhi

SIMON SPOTLIGHT

An imprint of Simon & Schuster Children's Publishing Division

1230 Avenue of the Americas, New York, New York 10020

This Simon Spotlight edition August 2023

Peanuts and all related titles, logos, and characters are trademarks of

Peanuts Worldwide LLC © 2023 Peanuts Worldwide LLC.

All rights reserved, including the right of reproduction in whole or in part in any form.

SIMON SPOTLIGHT, READY-TO-READ, and colophon are registered trademarks of

Simon & Schuster, Inc. For information about special discounts for bulk purchases,

please contact Simon & Schuster Special Sales at 1-866-506-1949 or

business@simonandschuster.com.

Manufactured in the United States of America 0723 LAK

10 9 8 7 6 5 4 3 2 1

ISBN 978-1-6659-4013-9 (hc)

ISBN 978-1-6659-4012-2 (pbk)

ISBN 978-1-6659-4014-6 (ebook)

Charlie Brown was excited.
It was going to be a fun day!
"There's nothing better than
a school fair, Sally," he told his sister.
"We should have one every day!"
Sally cheered.

Everyone was so excited about the fun day!
Everyone but Snoopy, that is.

It wasn't only the day of the school fair.

It was also the day of Snoopy's checkup at the vet.

Just then Sally noticed Snoopy
crawling on the ground.
"What's Snoopy up to?" Sally asked.

Charlie Brown sighed.
"I told him he has to go to the vet
for a checkup," he said. "And
Snoopy hates going to the vet!"

Snoopy ran as fast as he could.

He thought he had
successfully escaped.
But he ended up landing in a . . .
dunk tank!

Lucy was thrilled that
she had a volunteer.

"Hit the target and make a splash!"
she called out.

Snoopy looked at the target
and gulped.
He didn't *want* to make a
big splash!

Charlie Brown and Sally walked up
to Lucy.
"I guess I have time for one game,"
Charlie Brown said.

"Look!" Sally exclaimed.
"Snoopy is playing too."

"There he is!" Charlie Brown said, relieved. "I'll get him down."

Charlie Brown went in for the pitch. But the ball flew right over the dunk tank. Snoopy laughed.

"Let me try," Sally offered.
But she didn't hit the target either.

Just then Linus walked up to them.
"Ball, please," he said.
He wrapped the ball in his trusty
blanket and leaned in for the pitch.

"How are you going to hit anything, throwing a ball like *that*?" Lucy laughed.
But Linus knew he could always count on his blanket.
Snoopy landed in the dunk tank with a giant splash!

Charlie Brown and Sally walked
over to Snoopy.
"We had our fun. Now it is time to
go to the vet," he told Snoopy.

But Snoopy didn't listen.
He raced away.

Next Snoopy tried to disguise
himself with cotton candy.
It didn't work.

Then Snoopy hid in a bin of
stuffed bunnies.
Lucy was in for a big surprise when
she won a prize.
"We have a winner!" Marcie
announced.

Snoopy looked down sadly.
"I don't know what the big deal is,"
Charlie Brown told Snoopy.
"Your vet is very nice.
She always smiles and gives
you treats."

But again Snoopy didn't listen.
He snuck away from Charlie Brown
and hid in the fun house.

Charlie Brown found him
moments later.
"Come on!" Charlie Brown pleaded.
"We're going to be late for your
appointment!"

But Snoopy managed to
escape his leash!
"Good grief," Charlie Brown said.

Snoopy found a building that he
thought he could safely hide in.
But it turned out to be the
vet's office!
"Great job, Snoopy!" Charlie Brown
told him. "You ran straight to the vet!"

Soon it was time for Snoopy's
appointment.

"Snoopy is not afraid of a little
checkup," Charlie Brown told the vet.

"He is very brave!"

Snoopy bravely marched into his
appointment.
And before he knew it, it was over!

"See," Charlie Brown said.
"That wasn't so bad! I thought the
doctor was very nice.
She even gave you a treat!"

"We even have time to go back to the fair," Charlie Brown continued. "Although you *are* pretty dirty from running around. Maybe you should have a bath first." But Snoopy had had enough.
A bath could wait for another day!